5 Easy Pieces

More One-Act Plays

by Jason Milligan

A SAMUEL FRENCH ACTING EDITION

SAMUEL FRENCH

FOUNDED 1830

NEW YORK HOLLYWOOD LONDON TORONTO

SAMUELFRENCH.COM

ISBN 978-0-573-63389-8   Printed in U.S.A.   **#7135**

MUSIC USE NOTE

IMPORTANT BILLING AND CREDIT
REQUIREMENTS

FOREWORD

This is one of my most eclectic anthologies of short plays yet—chiefly because these pieces span so many different dramatic genres, ranging from the realistic and heartfelt (*RITUALS*) to the gritty and street-wise (*ONE WAY STREET*) to the eccentrically whimsical (*PAUL'S GHOST*), with an extra dose of broadly comic farce (*THE FIRE-BREATHING LADY AND THE SUGARPLUM FAIRY* and *KEY LIME PIE*) thrown in for good measure.

I'm quite fond of each of these plays for one reason or another ... they all reflect some corner of my creative playground. Most importantly for you, however, they're all very simple to produce—hence the title of this collection.

For each play, a few simple set pieces and props will easily identify the time and place so that focus can be placed on the characters and stories.

I truly hope you enjoy these plays.

Jason Milligan
Fall 2006

CONTENTS

For Madeline

RITUALS

by

Jason Milligan

RITUALS was originally commissioned by Primary Stages Company in New York City as part of their 2002 Short Play Festival, "A Moment of Bliss." The play was first performed on March 4, 2002 and was directed by Marvin Einhorn. The cast was as follows:

DAVE	Daniel Ahearn
PAT	Lisa Barnes
JANIE	Lucy McMichael

CHARACTERS

DAVE, early 40s

PAT, 40s

JANIE, late 30s

SETTING

A kitchen/living room
in a contemporary upscale condo.

The present.

(A tidy kitchen/living room in a contemporary upscale condo. At rise, the stage is dark. After a moment, DAVE, 40s, wearing a suit, enters and flips on the lights. He looks around, checks his watch, then exits again. The stage is empty for a few moments. He re-enters with PAT, 40s, a professional woman. An awkward silence for a moment, then:)

PAT. Nice place.

DAVE. Oh, thanks. *(Awkward pause.)* We always meant to re-model, you know. We were going to re-do the whole kitchen. New cabinets ... one of those islands in the middle here. I got this software that helps you lay out your own floor plan and everything. We just ... never got 'round to it. *(Pause.)* You know.

PAT. Yes.

(PAT checks her watch.)

DAVE. Ah ... could I get you something to drink? Coffee? I could make some coffee. Or some juice...

PAT. No, thank you.

(DAVE opens the fridge and looks in.)

DAVE. Just as well. We're all out of juice. Out of everything. Except... *(DAVE holds up a jar of jelly.)* You ought to see the hall closet. I should've bought stock in Costco. *(DAVE closes the refrigerator door, looks around.)* Is it warm enough in here?

PAT. Yes, thank you.

DAVE. Here ... sit down...

(DAVE gestures to a chair in the living room area. PAT takes off her coat and sits. She checks her watch again. DAVE checks his. Off-stage, we hear an ALARM CLOCK go off. DAVE starts to say

9

*something, but PAT just nods knowingly, as if to assure him that
it's not necessary to talk. DAVE wants to say something, but
holds back and nods. He stands, pacing. We hear a toilet FLUSH
offstage. DAVE anxiously checks his watch again. After a few
moments, JANIE, 39, enters, and goes to the fridge. She takes out
a jar of jelly and another of peanut butter. She opens a loaf of
bread and is about to start making a sandwich when she sees
DAVE.)*

JANIE. Oh. I thought you were— *(She suddenly sees PAT, whom
she doesn't know.)* —at work.

*(JANIE stares at PAT, who rises, goes to JANIE with a gracious
smile.)*

PAT. Hello. I'm—
DAVE. *(Explaining:)* Janie, this is Dr. Laufer. I've been telling
you about—
PAT. Pat Laufer. It's nice to meet you.

(PAT offers her hand. JANIE takes it, warily.)

JANIE. Dave?
DAVE. *(A gentle reminder:)* Don't act so surprised. I *told* you—
JANIE. I didn't realize—
DAVE. —I was going to bring her by—
JANIE. —you were going to spring this on me.
DAVE. We talked about this. We— *(Pause.)* Look, it's time to
deal with it. You said—
JANIE. —I know what I said! I'm dealing with it the best way I
know how! I'm—
DAVE. —making *lunches*, for chrissakes!
PAT. Dave? *(DAVE realizes that help is here at hand and steps
down. PAT steps forward, the cool, calm voice of reason.)* Janie, this
is meant to be a peaceful intervention. I'm not here to threaten you or
coerce you into doing anything against your will. Dave asked me
here—
JANIE. —what, to tell me I'm crazy?
DAVE. Those are your words, not mine.

PAT. *(To JANIE:)* No. To mediate, to—

DAVE. —to talk some sense into—

PAT. *(To DAVE:)* This is not helping.

DAVE. Well, *do* something, for chrissakes! The reason you came—

PAT. —was so that we could all try talking together. The three of us. *(Reassures JANIE:)* That's all we're going to do, is talk ... all right? *(Pause.)* I'm merely here to facilitate. I have no agenda. *(Pause.)* Look, if you'd rather I go, then I'll go.

(Pause. JANIE thinks about this, then:)

JANIE. I think ... I'd rather you go.

PAT. Are you sure?

JANIE. *(Pause.)* Yes.

PAT. All right ...

(PAT gets her coat and walks to the door.)

DAVE. Wait a minute ... you can't just leave!

PAT. She doesn't want me here. I told you, I wouldn't stay if—

DAVE. —but you can't go! You're supposed to—

PAT. I can't fix this for you, David. I told you that. I said I would mediate, if she were willing. She's not. *(Pause.)* Do you still want Wednesday at three?

DAVE. *(Eyeing JANIE:)* I dunno. We'll see.

PAT. Yes, well ... *(To JANIE:)* Good-bye.

(PAT goes. Silence.)

DAVE. Well, that was rude.

JANIE. *(Pause.)* Yes, it was.

DAVE. Driving her out of here like that ...?

JANIE. Oh, excuse me, I thought you meant sneaking her in here to ambush me when I got up—

DAVE. This has to stop.

JANIE. What do you mean?

DAVE. You know what I mean. This whole compulsive ritual, it's ridiculous!

JANIE. All right, so it's a ritual. Is it compulsive? I don't know. Is it *ridiculous*? You tell me. Hindu people believe in cremating the body. Did you know that? They carry the body around the funeral pyre exactly three times, then place it on the pyre. They believe that the soul of the dead transfers to another body after death. Now, I don't know about you, but to me, *that's* a little compulsive. I'm simply making sandwiches. I just—I have to *do* something. That's what this is all about for me, I have to be *doing* something.

DAVE. *(This is the whole problem:)* You still blame me.

JANIE. *(A tired topic:)* This is not about you, David.

DAVE. This is *all* about me! You still see this as my fault—

JANIE. —it's not your fault! All right? Yes, I wanted to keep him home that day, no, you didn't. We argued, you won. You took him. Some sick son of a bitch set off a bomb, six children dead and now ... *this (indicates the lunch)* is how I am coping. I am very aware of what I'm doing. I don't see how I'm harming anybody. Now, if you'll excuse me—

DAVE. Janie, I know you're hurting—

JANIE. How would you know?

DAVE. What, you think I don't feel anything?

JANIE. I don't know.

DAVE. We are different, you and I. It's easier for me *not* to talk about it. *Not* to have his pictures up, not to keep going through some ridiculous routine—

JANIE. —you can't erase him completely!

DAVE. I'm not try to erase him. But it's time to move on.

JANIE. That's what I'm trying to do! I just— *(She stops herself.)* Never mind.

(JANIE resumes making the sandwich.)

DAVE. This same wall. We always get to this same wall and it stops. Janie, something is terribly wrong, and—

JANIE. *Nothing's* wrong, all right?

DAVE. You're making lunch for a dead seven-year-old, I'd say a *lot's* wrong around here!

(JANIE suddenly hurls the bottle of jelly at the white wall and it shatters. The splatter of red where the bottle hit is unavoidable.)

JANIE. *(Explodes:)* I make lunch for him because that's all I have *left*! Yes, we have a photo album, but every day they seem more and more like pictures from someone else's life, places I never was, things I never did! Everything that we shared—that we did ... the walk to school, the walk back home, practicing his spelling, going to the zoo, bath time, story time, bedtime—those rituals made up the structure of our lives. But those don't make any sense now, without him. Like an equation and half the numbers are missing. The only ritual I have left that has any potency, any meaning for me, the only one imbued with a sense that there was even a life here at all, is *this* ... *(She indicates the lunch counter, then calms, more introspective.)* ... every morning, I was the first one up. Every morning, I made his lunch. The same thing, every day ... *(She holds up the jar of jam.)* It was a ritual that he wasn't a part of—something that I did on my own, but that still connected us somehow. *(Pause.)* The days are so long, so hard to get through, and this is the *only moment of pure joy* I have left. This is the only way I feel any kind of connection anymore ... you can call it ridiculous, you can call it insane, you can call it whatever you want, I really don't care—all I know is, it makes me feel how I used to feel. *(Pause.)* When he was still here. You don't understand it because you *want* to forget. I don't blame you, David. It's easier to forget. Much easier. But I would rather feel the pain and remember than to have no pain ... and forget. And that difference, David, that fundamental difference between us ... scares me. Because it keeps us apart. And it keeps us from healing.

(Long pause. DAVE looks at JANIE for a long while as tears well up in his eyes. Then he slowly walks across the kitchen and embraces her. A desperate embrace—as if she is giving him life itself.)

DAVE. Help *me* remember.

(Long pause. JANIE hands him the knife and he composes himself, goes to the counter and starts making a sandwich. JANIE watches him as we:
FADE TO BLACK.)

THE END

ONE WAY STREET

by

Jason Milligan

ONE WAY STREET was originally presented by The Grace Players at the Egyptian Arena Theatre in Hollywood as part of their "Acts of Grace" one-act play festival. The play opened on August 31, 1995 and was directed by Natalija Nogulich. The cast was as follows:

TERRY	Don Short
JOHN	Jack Rodgers
ARCH	Christopher Wynne

CHARACTERS

TERRY, a veteran cop, the interrogator, late 30s

ARCH, his partner, the middleman, early 30s

JOHN, a young cop, the opportunist, 20s

SETTING

Booth in the back of a coffee shop in Queens.

Ten o'clock at night.

The present.

(SETTING: Booth in the back of a neighborhood coffee shop, near the kitchen. Grease stains from generations past are visible on the wall. The place is old and has not been thoroughly scrubbed for quite some time.
AT RISE: ARCH, TERRY and JOHN sit in the booth, wearing police uniforms. ARCH and JOHN's jackets hang on hooks on either side of the booth and they are hunched over cups of coffee. TERRY wears his own jacket, having just entered a few moments ago. JOHN plays idly with the salt shaker and some sugar packets as we meet them in the midst of a hushed, urgent conversation:)

TERRY. ... how old are we talkin' here?
JOHN. Huh?
TERRY. How *old* was this broad 'xactly?
JOHN. I dunno.
TERRY. Take a guess, then. What? Sixty? Seventy?

(Pause. JOHN considers, then:)

JOHN. I dunno ... I think, more, like, ninety or somethin'.
ARCH. Ninety?
JOHN. Somethin' like that.
TERRY. So, in other words, it was her "time."
JOHN. I guess so. Yeah.
TERRY. I mean, if she was ninety ...
JOHN. Yeah, yeah.
TERRY. ... she musta known the Wright Brothers, for cryin' out loud.
JOHN. I dunno.
TERRY. So, what, then? She just dropped dead?
JOHN. Yeah. I dunno. Heart attack? How do old people die?
TERRY. *(Shrugs)* Heart attack.

ARCH. At's my guess.

JOHN. Okay, so, then, a heart attack.

ARCH. *(To TERRY:)* Hey, you want anything?

TERRY. Nah.

ARCH. *(To unseen waitress:)* We're fine. *(TERRY slips out of his coat.)* Oh, man. That's such a shame ...

JOHN. I know.

TERRY. What's a shame?

ARCH. This old lady.

TERRY. Oh.

JOHN. She was a nice old lady, too.

ARCH. Really?

JOHN. Yeah. Juanita.

TERRY. What?

JOHN. Huh? Oh, s'her name.

ARCH. "Juanita?"

JOHN. Yeah.

TERRY. What, she a Mexican broad?

JOHN. I don't think so.

TERRY. S'a Mexican name. Don't you know a Mexican name when you hear it? What, was this some old Mexican broad we're talkin' about?

JOHN. What difference does it make?

TERRY. I'm just askin'.

ARCH. Such a shame ...

TERRY. What?

ARCH. Nice old lady like that.

TERRY. *You* knew her?

ARCH. No.

TERRY. So then, what are *you* so sorry for?

ARCH. I dunno; an old lady dies like that; it's sad.

TERRY. "Sad?"

JOHN. Yeah.

TERRY. *(Suddenly remembering:)* What time is it?

ARCH. *(Looks at his watch:)* Ah ... ten.

TERRY. *(Rising:)* I gotta go.

ARCH. What?

TERRY. I got this game, 'cross town. I'm late.

ARCH. Wait, wait, Johnny said—tell him, Johnny.

JOHN. She had this—
TERRY. Wait a minute. Who? Had what?
JOHN. Juanita. She had—
TERRY. What? She had, "what?" I got this game, I gotta—

(TERRY gestures to the front door.)

ARCH. *(To JOHN:)* Tell him!
JOHN. ... she had this *safe.*

(Pause.)

TERRY. Okay. *(To ARCH, sinking back into his seat:)* Now we're getting someplace ...
JOHN. She was alla time tellin' me, "this neighborhood—"
ARCH. "—not what it used to be ..." Right?
JOHN. Yeah, yeah.
TERRY.Uh-huh ... so, what's in this safe?
JOHN. Well ... I don't know.
TERRY. You don't *know*?
JOHN. Well, yeah, sort of. She was alla time tellin' me how she had—
ARCH. —tell him!
JOHN. I'm tellin' him! I can't talk "faster" than I'm already talkin'! I'm tellin' him! I'm tellin' him!
ARCH. Okay, okay!
TERRY. So what's in this damn safe already? Jewelry?
JOHN. No.
TERRY. What, then? Cash?
JOHN. No.
TERRY. What?
JOHN. Gold bullion.

(Pause.)

TERRY. What?
ARCH. *(Savoring the words:)* "Gold bullion!"
TERRY. What was this old Mexican broad doin' with gold bullion?

ARCH. She wasn't Mexican.

TERRY. You knew her?

ARCH. No, but John said—

JOHN. Her husband.

TERRY. Huh?

JOHN. He salvaged this—I dunno—this ship.

TERRY. This what?

JOHN. "Ship." You know.

ARCH. What, like the Titanic or somethin'?

JOHN. No, some—

ARCH. They found the Titanic, y'know. I seen this "special—"

JOHN. No, no, this was, like, some Civil War ship or something, I dunno, coast of North Carolina—

ARCH. What, the Monitor? The Merrimack?

JOHN. I dunno, one a those things. *(To TERRY:)* He was the one, found it.

TERRY. When?

JOHN. I dunno. Long time ago.

ARCH. *(To TERRY:)* When he was young.

TERRY. Who? John?

ARCH. No, the husband!

TERRY. Whose husband?

ARCH. The old broad.

TERRY. *(Clarifying:)* The old Mexican broad.

ARCH. She ain't Mexican!

TERRY. You knew her?

ARCH. No—

TERRY. You ever *seen* her?

ARCH. No, but—

TERRY. Then how do *you* know? Huh?

JOHN. Her husband found the gold, back when *he* was young.

ARCH. In his "prime?"

JOHN. Whatever.

TERRY. So what's the story with this, what, this "ship?"

ARCH. He found it.

JOHN. The husband found it.

TERRY. Uh-huh. And where's the husband?

JOHN. He's dead.

TERRY. Dead?

ARCH. Wait a minute. Now I'm confused. What, they *both* had heart attacks?

TERRY. I thought you said she lived alone.

JOHN. She did, she did. *He* died a long time ago.

TERRY. When?

JOHN. I dunno.

TERRY. So, what, then? She killed him or somethin'? Is that what this is?

JOHN. No!

ARCH. Was *he* Mexican?

JOHN. I don't know.

ARCH. Where's the Mexican, then?

TERRY. Will you stop with the Mexican thing already!

ARCH. You're the one, said there was a Mexican in here someplace.

TERRY. *(To JOHN:)* Why are you telling me all this? Huh? There's some "point?" Huh? What? I got a game!

JOHN. He died, twenty years ago, I dunno, whatever. He died. But he left *her* the gold bullion.

ARCH. Poor old thing ...

TERRY. Why is she poor? She's got the gold bullion!

ARCH. But it's so sad ...

JOHN. Now, she's never spent any a this loot on account of, what?

ARCH. "Sentimental Value?"

JOHN. Right.

TERRY. *(To JOHN:)* S'at what she said?

JOHN. Yeah.

(TERRY digests this for a moment, then:)

TERRY. Okay, so go on. Go on ...

JOHN. Well, she's, like—I said, no friends. All of 'em, they've all died off ...

ARCH. You didn't tell me *that*!

JOHN. I didn't get to finish; he *(TERRY)* came in—

TERRY. He *(ARCH)* called me.

JOHN. ... nobody knows her anymore, I'm the only one, stops in to check on her.

ARCH. Any kids?

JOHN. No kids.

ARCH. Oh, my God, that poor, lonely old woman ...

JOHN. No meals on wheels, even. We're talkin' nothin' for this woman.

ARCH. No "meals on wheels?" What'd she eat?

JOHN. I dunno.

TERRY. Who cares what she ate, I wanna hear about the gold. *(To JOHN, trying to get back on track:)* So she's all alone ...?

JOHN. All alone.

TERRY. Except for you.

JOHN. Exactly. I'm on my beat, I drop by, you know, check "in" on her.

ARCH. Oh, man. My heart!

(ARCH clutches his heart as if he has heartburn.)

TERRY. It's the food in this place. Get some Tums.

ARCH. No, it's my heart breakin', hearin' about this old woman!

TERRY. *(Ignoring ARCH, to JOHN:)* So she's all alone in this house with, what, with all this—?

JOHN. Yes.

TERRY. —from North Carolina?

JOHN. Exactly.

ARCH. Tucked away in a safe.

JOHN. That's it.

(Pause.)

TERRY. How did the old Mexican guy get all that gold bullion here alla way from North Carolina?

JOHN. I dunno, he "brought" it here, I—

TERRY. Huh?

JOHN. I dunno!

ARCH. *He's* the Mexican?

JOHN. What? No! I don't know!

ARCH. He *(TERRY)* said he was Mexican.

TERRY. I don't know. Finish the story already!

JOHN. Well ... that's it.

(Pause.)

TERRY. That's *it*?

JOHN. Yeah.

TERRY. I'm missin' my game and that's all you got? *(To ARCH:)* You dragged me over here to listen to that?

ARCH. No, no—tell him about the safe.

TERRY. What about the safe?

JOHN. Well, she—

ARCH. It's—listen to this—

JOHN. She showed me the safe. One day, last July, s'hot as hell outside ...

ARCH. Oh, last summer was a ballbuster.

JOHN. —glass of "iced tea" or somethin', I dunno ...

ARCH. Hospitable?

JOHN. We're talking "very" hospitable.

ARCH. Very hospitable old lady. God, that's so sad ...

TERRY. Look ... get to the—

(TERRY takes ARCH's wrist, looks at his watch.)

JOHN. Okay, so she's, you know, "the neighborhood, it's gone right down the," blah, blah, blah, "back when I was your age," blah, blah, blah, "now I'm so afraid at night." You know. So then she takes me inna living room, takes me in there, and she shows me—

ARCH. —the safe!

JOHN. *(Not exactly:)* No ...

TERRY. What, then?

JOHN. A painting.

TERRY. A what?

JOHN. But there, *behind* the painting ...

TERRY. Aha!

ARCH. Just like inna movies! Hah! Hidden behind a painting, eh?

JOHN. Yeah.

TERRY. Can you believe it?!

ARCH. Was it a *real* painting?

JOHN. What?

ARCH. A "real" painting. You know—

JOHN. I dunno, it was ...

ARCH. —or was it a lithograph?

JOHN. I think it was real. It had brush strokes.

ARCH. Huh ...

TERRY. So, did she show you, you know, did she show you the combination?

JOHN. The—?

TERRY. Show you the—?

JOHN. That's the thing. She did it so fast, I didn't see it.

TERRY. But you *did* see the safe.

JOHN. Yes. I saw the safe.

ARCH. Was it signed?

JOHN. Huh?

ARCH. The painting. Was it—?

JOHN. I don't know, I wasn't evaluating the "art," look, we'll go over there, we'll see, all right?

TERRY. We'll—?

ARCH. Well, that's the Thing, see.

TERRY. What is?

ARCH. *(To JOHN:)* Tell him.

TERRY. *(To JOHN:)* What?

JOHN. Well, this old woman, she's dead, right?

TERRY. Right ...

ARCH. Heart attack.

JOHN. Yeah, whatever. But *nobody knows. (Pause. JOHN leans in for emphasis, lowers his voice:)* —not yet, anyway. Nobody else in the whole wide world knows that she's dead but us three at this booth.

(Pause. They look at each other.)

TERRY. Just us three?

JOHN. Yes.

TERRY. Just the three of us.

JOHN. Exactly.

ARCH. So then you're saying ... you found this old lady *today*?

JOHN. Around, I dunno, three o'clock this afternoon, yeah.

TERRY. On your "beat."

JOHN. Yeah.

TERRY. And you didn't call the coroner—?

JOHN. No.

TERRY. Why not?

JOHN. Well, because—

ARCH. *(Excited:)* Because he wanted to tell *us*—

TERRY. —no, no, I get that. I get it. But, I mean, why *us*? Huh? Why didn't you just—? You know.

JOHN. What, all by myself?

TERRY. Yeah.

ARCH. What, you mean, *him*? Go in there and—?

TERRY. Well, I mean, he's already in there, for chrissakes, he's standin' over the friggin' body, he's two feet away from the safe, for cryin' out loud, why didn't you just—?

JOHN. No, no, I *can't*, see, I—

TERRY. Why not?

JOHN. I don't know the first thing about crackin' a safe!

(Pause.)

ARCH. Oh.

JOHN. I mean ...

TERRY. So, the drift of it all is, you need somebody who can—?

JOHN. Yes.

(Pause; they look at each other.)

TERRY. Well, *we* don't know nothin' about crackin' a safe. I don't. *(To ARCH:)* Do you?

ARCH. No.

TERRY. So, what, then?

JOHN. I thought maybe you did.

TERRY. No.

JOHN. I thought maybe you could help me. I thought maybe we could, you know ... help each other. *(Pause.)* Three-way split.

TERRY. Hey, I told you: I don't know nothin' about crackin' safes. And I've missed my game now, thanks to you—

(TERRY gets up from the booth, grabs his jacket.)

JOHN. Wait a minute! You two collared that guy last year, re-

member? That guy, you know, that guy--
>ARCH. What, you mean that French guy?
>JOHN. Yeah!

(TERRY stops.)

>TERRY. Who? You mean that guy Rene?
>ARCH. That's him!
>JOHN. Yeah!
>TERRY. You heard about that bust?
>JOHN. Yeah.

(TERRY walks back to the booth, stands there.)

>TERRY. I think he's still in the joint.
>JOHN. In the—?
>TERRY. *(To ARCH:)* He's doin', what? Three years? I dunno.
He's still doin' time, ain't he?
>ARCH. I dunno, I think so, yeah ...
>TERRY. *(To JOHN:)* So?
>JOHN. So, can we see him?
>TERRY. See him?
>JOHN. Yeah.
>TERRY. *See* him?
>JOHN. I dunno. Yeah. "Talk" to him.
>TERRY. *Talk* to him?
>JOHN. Yeah.
>TERRY. What, we're gonna go out to the pen and ask him for
some "tips?"
>JOHN. I dunno, I—
>TERRY. What, then? "Hire" him? Three cops, we're gonna walk
into the joint and "hire" this guy to crack the old Mexican broad's
safe?
>JOHN. No. I dunno ...
>TERRY. What, then, Einstein?
>JOHN. Maybe we could just talk to him, I dunno.
>TERRY. Oh, so now we're back to "talkin'" to him.
>ARCH. *(To TERRY:)* Maybe you could talk to him, get him to—
>TERRY. No. No. I'm not goin' in there and askin' this guy for

anything. You got that? *(To ARCH:)* This is ridiculous.

JOHN. But I don't know how else to get into the safe!

ARCH. She died today? Sooner or later—

TERRY. What exactly you think's inside this safe, anyway? Huh?

JOHN. I told you!

ARCH. He told you. Gold bullion!

TERRY. Yeah, but have you actually seen it?

ARCH. No.

TERRY. I'm askin' him. *(To JOHN:)* You actually seen this gold bullion?

JOHN. *(Not really:)* Yeah.

TERRY. *(Let me get this straight:)* She opened the door to the safe up, let you look inside?

JOHN. *(Not a good liar:)* Yeah.

(TERRY looks at JOHN for a moment, then:)

TERRY. There's no gold bullion. He's full of crap, that's all. I gotta go, I got my game—

(TERRY starts to leave. JOHN rises.)

JOHN. No, wait a minute, she said—

TERRY. *(Wheeling around on JOHN:)* "She said, she said ..." It was some old broad, tryin' to get some attention outta you, and—

ARCH. —no, but she told him—

TERRY. —what, you soaked all this up like a sponge? It's all a bunch of crap. You're a crap sponge. Botha ya! Coupla crap sponges, I gotta find somebody who can wring both you out!

ARCH. I believe her!

TERRY. Oh, you do?

ARCH. Yeah.

TERRY. You believe her?

ARCH. Yeah.

TERRY. You ain't even met her!

ARCH. Well, I believe Johnny.

TERRY. Well, I don't. I think he's got an overactive imagination. And I think I'm done here.

(TERRY heads for the door.)

JOHN. She gave me *this*!

(JOHN takes out a handkerchief, unwraps a few vintage gold coins, lays them on the table. A long silence as TERRY walks back over and he and ARCH examine the coins. JOHN waits for a response.)

TERRY. Why didn't you tell us about this up front?
JOHN. I forgot.

(Long pause. TERRY stands where he is, then takes a step in closer and examines the coins closely. He sits down at the booth, leans right into JOHN, speaks in a hushed voice:)

TERRY. All right.
JOHN. All right, what?
TERRY. Tell me.
JOHN. Tell you what?
TERRY. What made you come to "us?"
JOHN. I dunno, I—
TERRY. What?
ARCH. I've known this kid a long time, Terry, I—
TERRY. I'm talkin' to the kid. *(To JOHN:)* What made you "bring" this to us?
JOHN. Like Arch said. I know him—
TERRY. —yeah, but you don't know *me*.
ARCH. I know you, Terry. I was the one who called.

(TERRY studies JOHN for a long time, then checks his pocket for change.)

TERRY. Anybody got a quarter? *(ARCH and JOHN both fish in their pockets. Each finds a quarter, each holds one up in offering to TERRY. TERRY studies both men, studies their quarters. Takes ARCH's quarter.)* I gotta make a phone call, tell 'em I'm not comin'. I'll be right back. *(TERRY starts out, calls as he goes:)* Order me a cup of coffee, will ya?

(TERRY goes. Pause.)

ARCH. I think it went well. I think it went very, very well.

JOHN. You do?

ARCH. ... as well as it coulda gone.

JOHN. I don't think he trusts me.

ARCH. Trust is a one way street.

JOHN. Huh?

ARCH. Once you get in with somebody, you're in. You know how it is. But you gotta get in with somebody first. Look, he don't know you yet. He'll get to know you.

JOHN. I dunno ...

(Pause.)

ARCH. Hey. You did the right thing. Callin' me. Me callin' him. We're doin' the right thing.

JOHN. I hope so.

ARCH. Trust me.

JOHN. 'Cause I, you know, I ain't never—

ARCH. I know.

JOHN. —nothin' like *this* before, y'know?

ARCH. I know.

JOHN. Not ever before.

ARCH. I know, I know.

(Pause.)

JOHN. You?

ARCH. What? *(JOHN looks levelly at ARCH. Yes:)* No!

JOHN. You haven't?

ARCH. No, no!

JOHN. I thought—

ARCH. Not me.

JOHN. I just figured—

ARCH. Uh-uh.

(Pause.)

JOHN. Who'd he go call again?

ARCH. These guys. You know, his game.

(Pause.)

> JOHN. You sure we can trust this guy?
> ARCH. I would trust him with my life.
> JOHN. Huh.
> ARCH. I swear, my life and soul. He said he wanted a cup a cof-
> fee?
> JOHN. Ah ... yeah.

(ARCH looks around for the waitress.)

> ARCH. Where is she?
> JOHN. I dunno, she may be on her break.

(ARCH looks for the waitress a moment, then:)

> ARCH. Okay, I'm gonna go to the can. She comes around, tell
> her one more coffee.
> JOHN. Okay.
> ARCH. And get me a refill, would ya?
> JOHN. Okay.

(ARCH rises, stops. Looks at JOHN.)

> ARCH. Hey. You did the right thing. Callin' me? You did the
> right thing.

(JOHN nods. ARCH goes. JOHN sits alone for a moment, fidgeting.
After a moment, TERRY returns. TERRY looks at JOHN a long
moment. JOHN holds his glance. TERRY finally sits across from
JOHN at the booth, then takes out a pack of cigarettes, lights one.
He holds eye contact with JOHN this whole time. TERRY pulls a
napkin out of the dispenser, takes a pen, hands it to JOHN, indi-
cating that he draw.)

> TERRY. Draw the house.
> JOHN. What do you mean?
> TERRY. I mean, draw the house.
> JOHN. You mean, like a "floor plan?"

TERRY. Yeah. A "floor plan." That's good. Yeah. *(JOHN starts to draw.)* I'm just wonderin' ... you ever done anything like this before, John?

JOHN. Ah ... no.

TERRY. You mean to say, you never been on the "take?"

JOHN. No.

TERRY. Not at all?

JOHN. No.

(An awkward pause. JOHN resumes drawing.)

TERRY. What made you call Archie?

JOHN. I needed some help with this.

TERRY. I know, but why *him*?

JOHN. I've known Arch since I was a kid. He looked after me after my Pop got killed.

TERRY. Your Pop got killed?

JOHN. Yeah, inna line of duty.

TERRY. Huh. *(Pause.)* So, were you the one, told Arch to call me?

JOHN. No. That was his idea.

TERRY. I was just curious.

JOHN. Oh.

TERRY. Keep drawin'. *(JOHN draws. TERRY takes a deep drag off the cigarette, watching JOHN closely. TERRY gestures to the drawing.)* Where's the safe?

JOHN. Ah ... *(JOHN locates it, draws it on the map.)* Here.

TERRY. Whassat, the dining room?

JOHN. Yeah.

TERRY. Uh-huh. *(Pause. JOHN draws.)* I thought you said the safe was in the living room.

(Pause.)

JOHN. Oh. Yeah. *(JOHN studies the drawing.)* You're right. It's—

(JOHN makes the correction on the drawing.)

TERRY. You know, I been on the Force for eleven years, John.

JOHN. Oh, yeah?

TERRY. Yeah. And all that time, nobody has ever pointed a finger at me. You hear what I'm saying?

JOHN. Yeah.

TERRY. Nobody has ever pointed a finger at me, said I was onna "take."

JOHN. Oh.

TERRY. What, does that "surprise" you?

JOHN. No.

TERRY. It doesn't surprise you?

JOHN. No.

TERRY. I'm just tellin' you, I'm clean, far's the department's concerned.

JOHN. That's good.

(Pause. TERRY studies JOHN for a moment, then:)

TERRY. Draw the house.

(JOHN draws. ARCH returns.)

ARCH. She's makin' some fresh coffee. *(TERRY nods, keeping his eye on JOHN.)* A fresh pot, it'll be a minute.

TERRY. Thanks. *(TERRY turns to ARCH, offers a cigarette.)* Want one?

ARCH. No, I told you, I quit. Remember?

TERRY. That's right. How long now?

ARCH. Ah ... two weeks.

TERRY. Two weeks. Wow.

ARCH. Yeah, Maureen bought me the patches. You know.

(ARCH indicates his upper arm.)

TERRY. That's good, that's good. Maybe I'll get some a those patches too. So, it was your idea to call me?

ARCH. No, it was John, asked me to.

(JOHN looks up. He and TERRY lock eyes in a tense stare down. Long, long pause.)

TERRY. *(Calmly and simply, to JOHN:)* There ain't no safe, is there?

JOHN. Yeah, it—

TERRY. *(Statement of fact:)* Don't lie to me. There ain't no safe.

ARCH. Terry. She showed him!

TERRY. There ain't no safe, Arch, and this kid—

ARCH. Look, I can vouch for him—

JOHN. She gave me the—

(JOHN gestures to the coins.)

ARCH. —known him since I was—

(TERRY suddenly leaps up from his seat, grabs JOHN's shirt front, and rips it open. The coins, the salt shaker, etc., go flying. JOHN tries to fight TERRY off, but TERRY is so fast and strong that he succeeds. We can now see, with his chest exposed, that JOHN is wearing a wire.)

TERRY. Look! You see?!

(TERRY slaps JOHN hard across the face.)

ARCH. *(Betrayed:)* Johnny!

(JOHN starts crying.)

TERRY. You piece of crap! What were you gonna get outta this, eh? Promotion?

JOHN. I—

TERRY. Huh? Well, to hell with your promotion. You got that? To hell with you!

ARCH. *(Disillusioned:)* Johnny ...

TERRY. *(Reassuring ARCH:)* He got nothin'. We didn't promise him anything, we didn't "say" anything. He got nothin'.

ARCH. How could you ...?

(JOHN is too ashamed to answer. TERRY rises, motions a calming gesture to the unseen waitress.)

TERRY. S'okay. Everything's okay … *(TERRY tosses a dollar bill on the table for his coffee, gets his jacket.)* I wanna see you show your face in the stationhouse again, s'what I wanna see. You good for nothing—what? You were gonna get your gold shield for this? You rat. Where is your loyalty? Where is your—?

(TERRY is consumed with anger, raises his arm as if he were going to beat JOHN.)

ARCH. Terry. Hey. Hey. Easy ...

(TERRY lowers his arm, looks at ARCH.)

TERRY. I'm goin'. You comin'? *(ARCH looks at JOHN again, just completely shocked at this turn of events.)* Well, I got a game. I'm late.

(TERRY turns and leaves. Long pause. JOHN can't face ARCH, he's staring at his lap, his crying is beginning to stop now.)

ARCH. How long I known you, Johnny?
JOHN. I'm sorry, Archie ...
ARCH. Huh? How long?
JOHN. I didn't *want* to do this ...
ARCH. No, but you want your gold shield. Is that it? Is that what this was? For—? *(JOHN nods.)* Man, you think you "know" some-body ... *(Pause.)* It's not like it used to be. People just out for themselves nowadays. Don't care who they hurt ...
JOHN. I never meant to hurt you, Arch, it was *him* they were after. They know he's crooked, they wanted to find some way to nail him. I never meant to hurt you.
ARCH. Yeah, well, it hurts alla same, Johnny. Bein' used like that.
JOHN. I'll make this up to you, I'll—
ARCH. What? How? How can you make this "up" to me? I can't trust you. You think I could ever trust you again? No way.
JOHN. I'm sorry!

(ARCH looks at JOHN, shakes his head.)

ARCH. You're "sorry?" That means nothing to me. I told you. One way street. You shoulda stayed *on* that street. 'Cause that's where people look out for you, people ... ah, what's the use? You wanted somethin', you didn't care who you stepped on. I hope you're happy. *(ARCH rises, throws a couple of dollars down on the table.)* I got your coffee. Don't call me anymore. And from now on ... stay on *your* side of the street.

(ARCH leaves. JOHN sits at the booth, pondering his fate as the lights slowly fade.)

END OF PLAY

PAUL'S GHOST

by

Jason Milligan

PAUL'S GHOST was originally presented as a staged reading at the George Street Playhouse on October 28, 1985, as part of the author's larger work, *Beatleplays*. The performance was directed by Casey Childs and the cast was as follows:

MAGGIE	Janet Reed
ANNE	Jessica Rausch
SHERRY	Roma Maffia

CHARACTERS

MAGGIE, eldest of the three teenage girls

ANNE, her best friend, naïve and trusting

SHERRY, their friend, the skeptic

HAL, Maggie's older stepbrother, the bully

SETTING

Maggie's kitchen in Oakland, California.

Ten o'clock at night.

December, 1969.

(SETTING: Late one night in December, 1969. Oakland, California ... although this story could—and, in some ways, <u>did</u>—happen all over the United States, during a mystical time when a global conspiracy of massive proportions was revealing itself to countless Americans.

AT RISE: Two teenage girls, MAGGIE and ANNE, sit at Maggie's kitchen table, studying the Beatles' "Abby Road" album cover.)

MAGGIE. ... see? They're walking away as if they're *leaving a cemetery*!

ANNE. Whoa, this is heavy ...

MAGGIE. ... John is the minister, y'see, he's all dressed in white ...

ANNE. ... so heavy ...

MAGGIE. Ringo is the undertaker ...

ANNE. ... because he's wearing black?

MAGGIE. Yes! Very good!

ANNE. What about George? He's wearing ordinary ol' clothes.

MAGGIE. *(Correction:) Work* clothes. Because *he* ... was the grave digger.

ANNE. *(Shivers:)* Whoa, this is, like, totally freaky!

MAGGIE. It gets even creepier! Paul is holding a cigarette in his *right* hand. But, as we all know, Paul McCartney is left-handed. And do you see the license plate in the background? "28 IF." Paul would've been 28 years old if he had lived.

ANNE. This is weirding me out, Maggie.

MAGGIE. *(Correction:)* Solitude.

ANNE. I mean, Solitude. So ... how did he die?

MAGGIE. Just follow the clues ... they're in the lyrics ... he blew his mind out in a car, on a Wednesday morning at five o'clock. He was driving and didn't notice that the lights had changed. So he was in a car crash ...

ANNE. ... and he lost his hair!

39

MAGGIE. Right!

ANNE. Okay, so ... if Paul *is* dead ... why'd the other three give us all these clues?

MAGGIE. Because! They want us to know!

ANNE. They do?

MAGGIE. Yes! They want us to "take our broken wings and learn to fly!"

ANNE. I thought that was about a bird.

MAGGIE. No. It's about us.

ANNE. How do *you* know all this?

MAGGIE. Because ... I have studied the clues. It's a global conspiracy. By the way, just in case anything suspicious happens to me, I've logged all of them in the back of my algebra notebook.

ANNE. I thought you were supposed to be doing algebra in your algebra notebook.

MAGGIE. No way! I am gonna be so famous when I finally prove the truth behind this story, I won't need to do algebra any more!

ANNE. Well, in the meantime, you're flunking out.

MAGGIE. You sound like my old man.

(SHERRY enters.)

MAGGIE. Enter, kindred spirit!

SHERRY. *(To ANNE:)* Why is she talking like that? *(To MAGGIE:)* Why are you talking like that?

MAGGIE. I'm just setting the mood, Moonbeam.

SHERRY. My name is not Moonbeam.

MAGGIE. Do you like Thistledown better?

SHERRY. I like *my* name. Sherry.

ANNE. Maggie thought we could all take funky, otherworldly names for the séance. She's gonna be Solitude and I'm gonna be Nightblossom ...

MAGGIE. *(To SHERRY:)* So, like, where is it?

SHERRY. Ah ...

MAGGIE. Don't tell me! You forgot it?

SHERRY. Not exactly ...

SOLITUDE. What do you mean, "not exactly?" Where is it?

SHERRY. *(Confesses:)* My brother took it to a slumber party over at Larry McGarry's house.

MAGGIE. No!

SHERRY. I told him that I needed it, and that made him want it even more!

MAGGIE. *(Suddenly suspicious:)* You didn't tell him about the clues, did you?

SHERRY. No, of course not, no! Remember? We took an oath! We pricked our fingers and everything!

(They all hold up their pinky fingers and inspect each other's.)

ANNE. Yeah, I know ... mine got a little infected. I told my mom I got caught in some rose bushes.

SHERRY. I'll get it back tomorrow—if he remembers to bring it home.

MAGGIE. That's too late. Tonight is the night. The moon is full ... the barometer's falling ... and the spirits are calling. We'll have to make our own instrument.

SHERRY. Our own what?

MAGGIE. Ouija board.

ANNE. Can we do that?

MAGGIE. We can do anything we want! My folks are away for the weekend and my stupid step-brother, who's supposed to be looking after me, took some stupid sorority girl to the drive-in.

ANNE. But what I mean is, if we make our own, will it work?

MAGGIE. Of course it'll work. The ones you buy are just cardboard and plastic anyway. It all depends on how sincere the seeker is. And we are nothing if not sincere. *(Down to business:)* Now, my Aunt Aurora mailed me specific instructions on how to make a homemade Ouija Board ...

SHERRY. If that's the case, then why were you pestering me to bring mine?

MAGGIE. I wanted an *official* one ... but not to worry, darklings. Here are Aurora's instructions ...

(She pulls out a folded-up piece of paper.)

ANNE. It kinda gives me the creeps when she calls us "darklings."

SHERRY. Yeah, like, why do you call us "darklings" anyway?

MAGGIE. It's a term my aunt uses.

ANNE. Is your aunt really a witch?

MAGGIE. Practically. Her official title is "spiritual advisor."

SHERRY. So, what, then ... she reads palms?

MAGGIE. *And* she sees signs. She can decipher the signs in tea leaves ... or the pattern of the stars in the cosmos ... she can even tell you what day you're going to die!

ANNE. *(Shivers:)* Oooh. I don't think I wanna know when I'm gonna die!

MAGGIE. Not to worry, Nightblossom. We're not seeking *your* fate this evening. Now, you know what a Ouija Board looks like ... write the alphabet across this piece of cardboard. A – Z, in two rows.

SHERRY. Right. And the sun is over on this side, with the word "yes" under it.

MAGGIE. Right. Which represents the Goddess of the Spirit World.

ANNE. Cool.

MAGGIE. And on the other side, the moon and the word "no." The moon is the God of the Spirit World.

SHERRY. Isn't it interesting that the woman says yes and the guy says no.

MAGGIE. *(Continuing to SHERRY:)* And remember to write 0 – 10 on there.

SHERRY. Underneath the alphabet. Okay. And then ... *(as she writes:)* "Good-bye."

MAGGIE. Make sure I can read it.

SHERRY. I will.

MAGGIE. 'Cause sometimes it's hard to read your writing.

SHERRY. I will! C'mon!

MAGGIE. Okay. Now, you, Anne—I mean, Nightblossom. You can help me make the message indicator.

ANNE. The what?

MAGGIE. The thing we all hold onto.

ANNE. Groovy. *(Pause.)* What can we make that out of?

MAGGIE. Well, let's see ... *(Looks around:)* We need something that stands on three legs ... here. This trivet should work.

ANNE. Yeah, but it's supposed to have an "eye" in the middle.

MAGGIE. I know ... and here's the eye.

(She takes out a scrap of dark velvet and unwraps it to reveal a glass eye.)

ANNE. Ooh, that's beautiful!

MAGGIE. It's a real glass eye, it was my grandpa's. He died and left it to my grandma, who gave it to my Aunt.

SHERRY. Yuck! That is disgusting!

MAGGIE. Keep drawing.

ANNE. How are you going to put the eye in there?

MAGGIE. The trivet has holes ... so I think it will fit if I just kind of wedge it in ... like this ... *(MAGGIE wedges the eyeball into a hole in the trivet, then holds it up.)* Voila.

ANNE. *(Shudders:)* That looks really freaky.

MAGGIE. Get used to it. A lot of things in the spirit world are freaky. *(To SHERRY:)* Are you done?

SHERRY. *(Handing over the hastily homemade board:)* Yes.

MAGGIE. Okay. All that remains is to turn on some mood music ... *(She turns on some sitar music.)* ... and light some candles ... *(She begins to light some candles. As she does:)* And, Moonbeam, if you'll turn out the lights? *(SHERRY obediently turns off the lights.)* And now ... let us gather around the spirit receptacle.

SHERRY. The what?

MAGGIE. The board.

ANNE. Do we all touch the message thingie now?

MAGGIE. Not yet. First, we listen ...

(Silence.)

ANNE. *(Pause, then whispered:)* What are we listening *for*?

MAGGIE. For the spirits ....

SHERRY. *(Pause.)* I don't hear anything.

MAGGIE. Exactly. As soon as it's completely silent, that's when the dead begin to speak.

ANNE. *(Nervous:)* What are they gonna say?

MAGGIE. All answers will be revealed.

ANNE. Can we turn a light on? I'm kinda freaking out here.

MAGGIE. Shhh.

ANNE. Maybe we should hold hands.

MAGGIE. Yes. By all means. Spirits flow through us ... like

electricity ...

SHERRY. Ugh. Yours is sweaty.

ANNE. Sorry.

MAGGIE. *(Calls out:)* Paul? Paul ... are you there? Do you hear us? We ask nothing ... we want nothing ... we seek nothing but the truth ... we have a question for you ...

ANNE. What are you gonna ask him?

SHERRY. Ask him if Bret Skyler is going to invite me to the prom.

ANNE. How would he know *that*?

SHERRY. I thought spirits knew everything.

MAGGIE. I'm not going to ask him that.

SHERRY. Why not?

MAGGIE. It might make him angry.

SHERRY. Angry?

MAGGIE. Perturbed. You have to be respectful of the spirits or they can become irritated.

SHERRY. I don't want any ghosts irritated at me.

ANNE. Paul wouldn't get irritated.

MAGGIE. *(Calls out, loudly:)* Paul? Paul! It is December 21, 1969 ... we have heard the news of your death and we need the truth ... we need to know ... we desperately need to know. We need ... to ... know ...

SHERRY. I think you've, like, made that clear.

MAGGIE. Shh. Will you be quiet? These transmissions have to travel a long way.

ANNE. How far?

MAGGIE. Far.

SHERRY. How far would that be in miles?

MAGGIE. Will you be quiet? I am the medium here.

ANNE. I thought we were all supposed to be holding the little thingie.

MAGGIE. We will, but spirits can only talk through one person at a time.

SHERRY. Says who?

MAGGIE. My Aunt Aurora. When she shoplifted all those bowl-ing balls, she said that the spirit of her ex-husband was inside of her, *making* her do it!

ANNE. *(Awed:)* Wow. *(Pause.)* So ... do you hear anything?

MAGGIE. *(Listens, then, disappointed:)* No ... nothing. So now we'll have to change our methods ... Let's all place our hands on the message indicator ... and be very still ... and listen ... *(They do, and all stare down intently at the board.)* Paul ... we need a confirmation of your passing ... we need your voice from the great beyond ... if you are indeed with the deceased, tell us now ...

ANNE. *(Reacting to a noise)* What was that?

SHERRY. My stomach. Sorry, I forgot to eat dinner.

MAGGIE. Paul ... tell us if you are truly in the land of the dead ...

(They all stare at the board. The pointer slowly moves.)

ANNE. It's moving ... it's *moving*!

MAGGIE. Shh!

SHERRY. *(Reads the letter that's shown:)* Y ...

ANNE. Oh my God ... It's moving again!

MAGGIE. Are you moving it?

ANNE. No! I thought *you* were!

MAGGIE. No!!

SHERRY. E ...

ANNE. Oh my God, I know what he's going to say!

MAGGIE. Shhh.

ANNE. Oh my God!

MAGGIE. ...T. *(Pause.)* "Yet?"

ANNE. No, he meant "yes." He *must've* said yes!

SHERRY. No, I think he said—

MAGGIE. He said "Yet."

ANNE. That doesn't make any sense.

SHERRY. Actually ... he said "Yei." *(Pause.)* That's not a "T" ... it's an "I."

ANNE. *(Squints at the board:)* Well, it's a very squiggly "I".

MAGGIE. *(To SHERRY:)* I *knew* we wouldn't be able to read your writing. And look, you've got the letters out of order—that's why he got thrown off!

SHERRY. You didn't say what *order* they had to be in!

ANNE. "Yei?" What does "yei" even mean?

MAGGIE. I think it might just be ... the Tibetan word for yes!

SHERRY. Really?

MAGGIE. Yes! I mean, "Yei!"

SHERRY. How would you know Tibetan?

MAGGIE. I sense it! He's telling us "yes!" Paul! Paul, you who speaks from beyond the grave, appear to us now!

ANNE. No!

MAGGIE. Shhh!

ANNE. What if he looks like something out of "Night of the Living Dead?"

MAGGIE. Paul ... appear to us now!

ANNE. No, Paul! Don't! Stay where you are!

MAGGIE. Don't interrupt.

ANNE. I'm sorry, this is just freaking me out!

MAGGIE. Paul! Appear!

(An enormous dark shadow suddenly drifts up onto the wall behind them. They shiver as they watch it. They begin to draw together, to huddle for safety as the shadow grows ... grows ... and then – the door flings open to reveal HAL, Maggie's older brother, standing in the doorway.)

HAL. What are you freaks doing?

MAGGIE. *(Coldly:)* Oh, it's only you.

ANNE. *(Who has a crush on him:)* Hi, Hal.

HAL. Hi, Amy.

ANNE. *(Correcting him:)* Anne. But you can call me Amy, if you want to. How's college life?

HAL. Cool. How is nerdy high school life?

(ANNE wilts at this comment.)

MAGGIE. Thanks a lot, Hal ... you totally scared us!

HAL. What's going on here?

MAGGIE. Nothing.

HAL. *(Looks around, realizes:)* ... a séance?

MAGGIE. Don't be ridiculous!

HAL. Then what are you doing in here? With all these candles and this music and—what are you doing?

MAGGIE. Why do you keep asking me that? I should be asking you, what are *you* doing here? You're supposed to be at the drive-in with some sorority girl.

HAL. Oh. She ate a bad hotdog and threw up all over my dash board in the middle of *The Ghost and Mr. Chicken.* I don't even know how it ends!

ANNE. I heard Mr. Chicken meets the ghost.

HAL. *(Sees the homemade board.)* You guys have got ghosts on the brain! *(He picks up the handmade board.)* Hah! You don't even know how to spell it. It's "Ouija," not "Ouiji." Man, you chicks are so square.

MAGGIE. *(Snatching it away:)* Give it here.

HAL. Who were you trying to talk to?

MAGGIE. Nobody. Leave us alone.

HAL. Your mom?

MAGGIE. Stop it. Right now!

SHERRY. *(To ANNE:)* Actually ... it's late. We'd better get going.

ANNE. But—

SHERRY. *(Whispered urgently:)* Get your things and let's get out of here!

(They rise and begin to pick up their jackets, purses, etc.)

HAL. Was this more of your Aunt Agnes' nonsense? I don't know why you listen to her anyway.

MAGGIE. Because she's a genius. She's enlightened. And her name is Aurora.

HAL. "Aurora." Yeah, right. That's just one of her aliases.

ANNE. Her what?

SHERRY. Never mind, we need to get home ... 'bye Maggie, we'll call you tomorrow.

ANNE. 'Bye Hal—

SHERRY. *(Shoving ANNE out the door:)* C'mon!

(They are gone.)

MAGGIE. Thanks for driving my friends off. And a great big extra huge thank you for insulting my Aunt Aurora in front of them!

HAL. Ugh, if I have to hear her name one more time ... she's a fake! Do you honestly think, if she was so great at getting advice from the spirit world, that she'd be in jail right now? I would think the spirits would have warned her, they'd have said, "the fuzz is coming, book outta there, baby," before she got caught.

MAGGIE. She has a tremendous gift!

HAL. Wait a minute ...*(Picks up a record album and holds it up:)* Don't tell me ... were you calling Paul McCartney from the grave?

MAGGIE. No!?

HAL. You liar! I read about it in your algebra book. I know all about your lame-o conspiracy theories—

MAGGIE. Oooh! I can't *believe* this! You went through my stuff?!

HAL. Well, you leave it all over the house!

MAGGIE. So? It's my house!

HAL. No, it's *my* house! You're just lucky that there as an extra room—

MAGGIE. Shut up!

HAL. You're lucky that my mom fell all over your square old dad—

MAGGIE. He is not square!

HAL. I dunno why she even digs him! They're total opposites!

MAGGIE. Yeah? Well, you and me are too! I'm caring and sensitive and you're nasty and mean—

HAL. I am not!

MAGGIE. You are! You're sadistic and cruel to me, day and night—

HAL. —well, do you blame me?! Everybody fawns all over *you*! Everybody's always checking in to see "how Maggie is." "Maggie lost her mom, you know, I hope she's okay," "Poor Maggie," everybody's always so worried about Maggie, well, what about *me*?! But three years ago, my dad leaves for Vietnam, and ...

(He stops himself, fighting back tears.)

MAGGIE. *(Quiet and caring:)* I know.

HAL. No, you don't. Nobody knows! Mom just pretends like he never even existed, all she can talk about is *your* dad! And meanwhile, he's gone! Gone! I've got this pain inside that never goes away!

MAGGIE. I know what you feel.

HAL. You don't know!

MAGGIE. Hal. I know.

*(She goes to him and embraces him. He begins to sob and clutches
    her tightly.
Lights slowly fade to black.)*

THE END

THE FIRE-BREATHING LADY AND THE SUGARPLUM FAIRY

by

Jason Milligan

THE FIRE-BREATHING LADY AND THE SUGARPLUM FAIRY
was originally presented as a staged reading by the Grace Players at
the Egyptian Arena Theatre in Hollywood, Natalija Nogulich, artistic
director. The play was originally presented on December 9, 1995 and
directed by Stefanie Milligan. The cast was as follows:

GLORIA	Kathleen Walker
JIM	Tom Overmyer
BELINDA	Bess Walker
GUS	Guy Walker
BILLY	Tim Walker
BOB	Tom Parks
ANNIE	Ashley Myers
PIZZA BOY	Tim Myers

CHARACTERS

GLORIA BOUVIER, an overbearing Southern stage mother

JIM CLARK, a teacher at an elementary school

BELINDA, Gloria's 10-year-old daughter

GUS, Gloria's 8-year-old son

BILLY, Gloria's 12-year-old son

BOB, Gloria's husband

ANNIE, the babysitter

PIZZA BOY, a poor young soul trapped in the middle

SETTING

The Bouvier living room.

Christmas eve.

The present.

(SETTING: The living room of the Bouvier home. Christmas eve, the present.

AT RISE: JIM CLARK stands in the doorway wearing a down jacket and a wool knit cap. GLORIA BOUVIER, a Southern woman of tremendous animation and ambition, stands before him. Her 8-year-old son, GUS, is crouched under a Christmas tree upstage, peeking into every package under the tree. Music from the Nutcracker plays in the background. Gloria's daughter BELINDA does gymnastics—flips, headstands, etc., throughout the play. The child never stops. GLORIA snaps an endless stream of snapshots of her daughter with a camera. We should sense a household out of control ...)

JIM. ... you can't be serious.
GLORIA. ... as a traffic accident. Hold it right there, Belinda.

(BELINDA poses. GLORIA snaps a photo.)

JIM. You can't withhold performers ... and you can't "boycott" a school play!
GLORIA. You act as if I'm behaving in a criminal manner. I'm merely trying to stand on principle. You see, my mother, God bless her, always taught me to stand on principle.
JIM. Principle? *What* principle? You wanted your daughter to get a big part, and she's in the chorus. I can't make everybody happy. Now get her dressed, and let's get her down to the school. The curtain goes up in ... *(checks watch)* fifty minutes.
GLORIA. Just watch her, Mr. Clark. Please, just watch her!

(They watch her for a moment, GLORIA in awed silence, JIM in exasperation.)

JIM. Yeah, great. You got a 10-year-old Agnes DeMille on your hands. Where's Billy? We've got to go!

GLORIA. I don't think you understand—

JIM. Oh, I understand all right. You're *crazy*! But I want you to know, I am a professional. I have staged ballets when the power went out and we had to work entirely in candlelight. I have presented outdoor operas under the worst weather conditions known to man! I am not about to let you stop me. I have a show to put on, and your daughter is in the chorus, and your son is playing the lead!

(BILLY enters, wearing part of his Prince uniform. Tights, jacket, et al.)

BILLY. I'm not going!

GLORIA. What do you mean, you're not going? Of course you're going, honey, you're the star!

BILLY. I'm not gonna get up in front of people in these stupid tights! All the guys are gonna laugh at me! I won't do it! I won't! I won't! I won't!!!

(BILLY runs off. BELINDA continues her handstands, et al. GLORIA snaps a photo.)

GLORIA. Isn't she a Little Star?

JIM. Five hundred watts ... Look, you wanna play Extortionist Stage Mother? Fine. Then I don't need her. She's out of the show, and you're the one to thank. One little space on the back row, who's gonna notice? One less Fairy in the chorus, who's gonna care? I hope you're happy. Now if you'll excuse me, I have a show to put on ...

(JIM starts for the door.)

GLORIA. If you leave now, you'll be leaving without my son. *(JIM stops in his tracks. He forgot about this minor detail.)* You *have* to have my son, don't you? He's the only boy in the entire school who knows all the steps. Because in 48 minutes the curtain is going up, and if there isn't a Prince in the Nutcracker, you know what you'll get for Christmas, Mr. Clark? Something papyrus and pink and crisp. A pink slip. You should know by now that people around here take their Christmas plays *very* seriously. *(JIM takes a slug from a Maalox bot-*

tle.) You see, I learned many lessons about negotiating from my grandmother. Did I ever tell you that my grandmother was a performer? A very *gifted* performer. *(To BELINDA:)* Keep your back straight, dear.

JIM. Okay, look. The next show, I promise, the next show your daughter will have—

GLORIA. "A role of substance." That's what you promised me *this* time, young man, and the third snowflake fairy from the left on the back row is not what I consider a "role of substance."

JIM. You don't understand—

GLORIA. Oh, I understand perfectly, Mr. Clark. You have lied to me! Betrayed me. Just like Ignatius Crofford.

JIM. Who?

GLORIA. The ringmaster!

JIM. What are you talking about?

GLORIA. My grandmother could breathe fire!

JIM. And they say there's no such thing as heredity ...

GLORIA. She was the greatest female fire breather of the 20th Century! Mr. Ignatius Crofford booked her in quite a few of his circuses—the more affluent circuses—during the Depression.

(BILLY enters.)

BILLY. I won't wear it, Mom. I won't. I swear, I'll jump out the window before I go down there looking like this!

GLORIA. ONCE AND FOR ALL, YOUNG MAN, YOU WILL WEAR IT, AND YOU WILL LIKE IT! AND DON'T YOU DARE JUMP OUT THAT WINDOW, OR I'LL WRING YOUR LITTLE NECK, YOU HEAR ME? *(BILLY leaves. GLORIA notices GUS for the first time.)* And *you*! Get out of those presents right this instant, before I tell Santa what an evil, ungrateful little MOLE you are and he brings you a tub of ear wax for Christmas!

(GUS runs out.)

JIM. Look. I haven't got time to—

GLORIA. —just *watch* her, Mr. Clark. She's been practicing. Like any good understudy. Show him, dear. Show him the dance of the Sugarplum Fairy. *(BELINDA does a cartwheel.)* No, dear. The dance. Of the Sugarplum Fairy. *(BELINDA, with some prepping from Gloria, does a few steps. They're not great.)* You see? She has natural talent, Mr. Clark. A child with natural talent and charisma. I don't know where she gets it from. Not from me, Lord knows I don't have a talented bone in my whole body. And certainly not from Bob ...

(BOB, Gloria's husband, enters.)

BOB. Is there anything to eat in this house?

GLORIA. DO I LOOK LIKE A *GROCER*? Is my name Piggly-Wiggly?

BOB. Honey, I'm starvin'. I just wanted a little somethin' to eat before we go down to the school. Last time you got all mad because my stomach was growling so loud and everybody was looking over ...

GLORIA. Open a can of Vienna Sausages, then. Something. Fend for yourself, Bob! Please? For once in your life? I am trying to deal with your daughter's future here! *(BOB blinks twice, leaves. BELINDA continues doing her dance step. GUS, unnoticed, re-emerges and continues opening presents. GLORIA takes out an aspirin bottle and washes a couple of tablets down.)* My head is splitting. *Splitting.* You have no idea ...

JIM. Look, Mrs. Bouvier—

GLORIA. It's pronounced like the French, Mr. Clark. "Boo-vee-ay." As in Jackie, before she met JFK.

JIM. —let's work something out here. Because you're right, without your son as the Prince, I don't have a play, and I'm supposed to have a play in ... *(checks watch)* forty-one minutes.

GLORIA. Mm-hmm ... Well, just how badly do you want him?

JIM. What?

GLORIA. How badly do you want him?

(GLORIA strikes a seductive pose.)

JIM. Are you trying to seduce me, Mrs. Bouvier?

GLORIA. *(Moving in very close and whispering passionately:)* This is a matter of life and death, Mr. Clark.

JIM. WHAT LIFE AND DEATH? IT'S A PLAY! A FRIGGIN' SCHOOL PLAY!!

(GLORIA grabs JIM, kisses him furiously. BOB enters. Jim breaks away.)

BOB. There are no Vienna Sausages.

GLORIA. What?

BOB. I looked in every cabinet, there are no Vienna Sausages anywhere!

GLORIA. Then boil a hot dog.

BOB. I don't see any hot dogs, either. I don't see anything except some cat food.

GLORIA. People in India who are starving to death would be thrilled to get some cat food! But you! All you ever do is complain!

BOB. There's gotta be *some*thing to eat in this house ...

(BOB exits.)

GLORIA. *(To BELINDA:)* THAT IS ENOUGH! STOP IT, OR YOU'LL RUIN YOUR ARCHES!

(BELINDA shrugs, goes back to her handstands.)

JIM. You've got to understand, there are certain political forces at work here, Mrs. Bouvier ...

GLORIA. Political forces ...?

JIM. I—I *had* to cast Alicia Jones as the Sugarplum Fairy!

GLORIA. The child with a face like a horse.

JIM. She does not have a face like a horse.

GLORIA. A donkey, then.

JIM. She's getting braces.

GLORIA. What she *needs* is plastic surgery.

JIM. The point is ... *(A confession:)* Her father owns a roofing business in town, and, well ...

(He makes a gesture, which is supposed to finish the sentence. GLORIA looks at him a moment, then gets it.)

GLORIA. OH! Now it's coming clear! The Writing on the Wall! Avarice and deceit!

JIM. No avarice! I just need a new roof on my house, I'm tired of buckets and pots and pans and bowls catching all the water every time it rains!

(BOB enters with a can of Spam.)

BOB. I found some Spam.
GLORIA. THEN EAT IT! EAT YOUR SPAM!
BOB. It's expired.
GLORIA. What?
BOB. It's a year old.
GLORIA. What's the worst thing that can happen? A little case of ptomaine? Tell your daughter how beautiful she is.
BOB. *(Mechanical:)* You're beautiful, baby.

(BOB goes.)

JIM. Look. I'll level with you, Mrs. Bouvier. It's not that your daughter isn't talented ...
GLORIA. Oh, Lord. I hear it coming. Just like my grand-mother ...
JIM. What?
GLORIA. They replaced her with a Sword Swallower! Can you imagine how crushing that was for her? A common Sword Swal-lower! *She* had talent. She could breathe fire!

(GLORIA breathes on JIM, as if breathing fire.)

JIM. Look. I don't want any bad blood between us, Mrs. Bouvier. So I tell you what I'm gonna do ... I'll have *two* Sugarplum Fairies in the show. All right? Your daughter ... and Alicia Jones. How's that sound?

(BILLY enters.)

BILLY. I'm not going.
GLORIA. BACK IN YOUR ROOM! NOW! Or you'll be sleep-ing in the trunk of the car again tonight! *(To GUS:)* You too! NOW! *(BILLY and GUS leave.)* Ow. My head ... it feels like a big kettle drum. Even my *hair* is throbbing. Have you ever had a day like that,

Mr. Clark? When your hair throbbed?

JIM. I think I'm having one right now ... *(GLORIA downs two more aspirin.)* Are you with me, Mrs. Bouvier? Two Sugarplum Fairies. That's the best I can do.

GLORIA. Two?

JIM. Yes.

(She studies JIM, looks at her daughter a moment, then back at JIM:)

GLORIA. *One.*

JIM. Mrs. Bouvier—

(The doorbell rings. GLORIA goes to answer it. GUS re-enters and returns to the presents. GLORIA lets ANNIE, the babysitter, in.)

GLORIA. Annie! Oh, good. We're just about to leave ...

JIM. We are? I'm a little lost here. Define "we" ...

ANNIE. What time will you be home tonight?

GLORIA. Around nine.

ANNIE. Can I use your phone?

GLORIA. Yes. You'll be babysitting for Gus tonight ... where is Gus? *(GUS's head pops up.)* There you are, you little demon! In your room! Now! Or you'll be sleeping in the trunk of the car again tonight! *(Pause.)* No, you can't sleep in the trunk, Billy's sleeping in the trunk ...

(ANNIE dials the phone as GLORIA downs some more aspirin.)

JIM. Billy can't sleep in the trunk, Mrs. Bouvier. I need him on stage in ... *(checks watch)* thirty-seven minutes!

ANNIE. *(Into phone:)* Hello? Cheryl? Yeah, come on over. They're just about to leave, and they'll be out till nine ...

(ANNIE hangs up, dials another number.)

JIM. Please, Mrs. Bouvier—

GLORIA. You can go for one winter without a roof on your house. You said yourself, you have plenty of pots and pans to catch the drips. But can my child go without the experience of a lifetime?

Would you stand there and deny her the experience of her little life-time?

(GLORIA cues BELINDA, who looks over pitifully.)

JIM. Playing the Sugarplum Fairy at Elk Grove Elementary is not what I'd call the experience of a lifetime!

GLORIA. Don't you tell me what is and is not the experience of my daughter's lifetime, Mr. Clark! I, and I alone will determine what the experiences of her lifetime are! *(The doorbell rings.)* Goodness me, now what?

(GLORIA answers the door. A PIZZA DELIVERY BOY stands there, out of breath. JIM pours some bourbon from a pocket pint into his Maalox, shakes it up, slugs some down.)

PIZZA BOY. Twelve minutes!

GLORIA. Excuse me?

PIZZA BOY. I made it in twelve minutes!

ANNIE. *(Into phone:)* Is Daryl there ...?

GLORIA. Who are you?

PIZZA BOY. *(Fighting for his breath:)* Jeff!

GLORIA. Do you have some ... purpose, young man?

PIZZA BOY. Somebody ordered a pizza. Fifteen minutes, or it's half-price. I made it in twelve!

GLORIA. No one here ordered a pizza.

PIZZA BOY. *(Hopefully:)* Extra anchovies?

ANNIE. *(Into phone:)* ... they'll be out till around nine.

GLORIA. *(Crossing to ANNIE:)* Annie, did you order a pizza?

ANNIE. No ma'am.

GLORIA. I commend you on your speed, young man, but no one ordered a pizza.

PIZZA BOY. Oh, man ... *(To JIM:)* If they find out, this comes out of my pay!

JIM. *(To the PIZZA BOY:)* Jeff, isn't it? *(The PIZZA BOY nods.)* My advice to you, Jeff? Pay for that pizza out of your own pocket, and *never tell a soul!*

PIZZA BOY. *(Surprised by the force of Jim's passion:)* What??

JIM. Don't you *ever* let 'em find out! 'Cause, trust me, Jeff, one little indiscretion, and—boom! You wind up just like me ... *(He gestures to GLORIA, who is busy with BELINDA at the other end of the room.) ... putting on school plays!* I thought it was just some big cliché, you know, "you'll never work in this town again!"

ANNIE. Is Carla there ...?

JIM. I thought I was invincible, I mean, there I was, working on Broadway, for cryin' out loud! *How was I supposed to know that I had fallen for the producer's wife?*

GLORIA. Mr. Clark, if we have no further business to discuss, I suppose you'll be going, then. I'm sorry we couldn't reach an agreement. I had so wanted to work with you.

(JIM looks at GLORIA; looks at the PIZZA BOY. Considers his plight. Then:)

JIM. OKAY! OKAY! YOU WIN!! Belinda is the lead Sugarplum Fairy, all right?

GLORIA. Belinda! Did you hear? Congratulations! Aren't you thrilled? *(BELINDA shrugs. Calling off:)* Billy! Get your things together! We're leaving!

(BILLY enters.)

BILLY. I won't do it. I won't. I won't go down there like this!

JIM. If he doesn't go on, Belinda doesn't go on!

(GLORIA thinks for a moment, then:)

GLORIA. *(To BILLY:)* All right. Change into your baseball uniform.

BILLY. Yay!

(BILLY runs off.)

ANNIE. *(Into phone:)* Is Debbie there ...?

GLORIA. *(To JIM, an order:)* He can wear his baseball uniform.

JIM. No he can't! He's the Prince! He can't wear a baseball uniform! He—wait a minute, who's DIRECTING THIS PLAY? THIS IS MY PLAY!! I'M NOT SOME NOVICE, I KNOW WHAT I'M DO-

ING! I'M A PROFESSIONAL!!!

ANNIE. ... they're just leaving now, and they'll be out till nine. Yeah. See ya.

(ANNIE dials another number.)

PIZZA BOY. What am I supposed to do with this pizza?
GLORIA. Take it away, please.

(The PIZZA BOY leaves. BILLY enters, in baseball uniform, tossing ball up and catching it in his mitt.)

GLORIA. You won't regret this, Mr. Clark. And now that we've got a working relationship established, things should be much simpler when the Easter Pageant comes around ...

(JIM drops his head in his hands. GUS enters and resumes opening presents.)

ANNIE. *(Into phone:)* Is Carmelina home? It's Annie ...
GLORIA. Well, then. Are we all ready?

(BOB enters.)

BOB. Has my pizza come yet? I'm starving.

(Music from the Nutcracker booms over the sound system as we go quickly to black.)

THE END

KEY LIME PIE

by

Jason Milligan

CHARACTERS

CHARLENE, a nervous Southern woman, mid-twenties
TRICIA, her older sister
ARCHIBALD STOKES, an elderly man
NURSE

SETTING

A small Southern town.
The present.

Scene 1

(SETTING: Suggestion of a kitchen in TRICIA's apartment in a small Southern town in the present.

AT RISE: The stage is empty. CHARLENE, TRICIA's younger sister, rushes in madly, drops her purse, then stops, staring at four key lime pies on the kitchen table. She then catches her breath, rushes to the silverware drawer, takes a fork from it, and begins raking feverishly through the pies with the fork, one at a time. After a few moments of this, TRICIA enters, wearing a wedding dress and looking very angry. CHARLENE looks up from her messy activity and sees TRICIA.)

TRICIA. *(Fuming:)* Well?
CHARLENE. I don't know yet ...

(CHARLENE has finished number two by now, turns to number three.)

TRICIA. You'd *better* find it.
CHARLENE. I will. I swear I will ...
TRICIA. You'd better! *(Digs a cigarette out of her purse, lights it.)* Oooh, this was the wrong week to stop smoking ...

(CHARLENE has finished number three. She takes a breath, prepares herself, then launches in on number four. TRICIA watches. Very soon it's apparent that, whatever they're looking for, it's not there. TRICIA exhales a long, tense breath. Pause.)

CHARLENE. I'm sorry!
TRICIA. Stop saying that! I swear, if you say you're sorry one more time, I don't know what I'll DO!

CHARLENE. I'm s— *(CHARLENE stops herself.)* Okay. Look. I made a mistake. I apologize. *(Down to business:)* What do we do now?

TRICIA. Now?

CHARLENE. Yes!

TRICIA. How should I know?

CHARLENE. Tell me what to do, Tricia! I wanna *fix* this!

TRICIA. You can't fix this! How can you FIX this? This was supposed to be MY DAY and you've ruined EVERYTHING!

CHARLENE. It's STILL your day, Tricia! It IS!

TRICIA. This day only comes around ONCE in your life, Charlene.

CHARLENE. It came around six times for Momma.

TRICIA. Our Mother is an IDIOT, Charlene! She— *(Regulating her breathing:)* I must stay calm ... I must stay calm ... *(Pulling herself together.)* Okay. Okay ... how many were there all together?

CHARLENE. Twelve.

TRICIA. And you sold—how many?

CHARLENE. I made four for your wedding and sold eight at the Christian Women's Bake Sale yesterday.

TRICIA. Do you remember who all you sold them to?

CHARLENE. Who all I—? *(Shrugs.)* Probably.

TRICIA. Good!

(TRICIA hands her the phonebook.)

CHARLENE. What's this?

TRICIA. What's it look like? It's the phonebook.

CHARLENE. What're we gonna do?

TRICIA. *You* are gonna look up each and every one o' those people and you're gonna ask them if they've got it!

CHARLENE. Oh, Tricia! I can't do that! I'll *die* of embarrassment!

TRICIA. Either you die of embarrassment, or I'll KILL YOU!

CHARLENE. Tricia, don't be so mean!

TRICIA. Mean? What do you expect, Charlene? I'm supposed to be getting married in two hours!

CHARLENE. Here, use my class ring— *(But she can't get it off)*

TRICIA. I DON'T WANT YOUR CLASS RING, CHARLENE!

DON'T YOU UNDERSTAND? I WANT MY RING! *MY* RING! All my life, you're the one who's gotten EVERYTHING! The YOUNGER one! The SPOILED one! I've always had to fend for myself while Daddy gave you everything and now, here we are on MY SPECIAL DAY and thanks to YOU, I don't even have a WEDDING RING ...

(TRICIA trails off into sobs. CHARLENE grabs the phonebook.)

CHARLENE. Okay. Okay! I'll call 'em. Every single one of 'em. We'll get your ring back, I swear we will! *(Opens the phonebook, looking.)* Crayola Rutherford bought one. I'll call her first. *(Dials the phone. Waits as it rings.)* Hi. Miz Rutherford? Hello. This is Charlene Wynn. Charlene Wynn? *(Pause.)* Tricia Wynn's little sister? Uh-huh. How're you? *(Pause.)* Well, reason I'm calling is, you bought a pie from me yest'day at the Sheldon County Christian Women's Bake Sale. Yes'm. Key lime pie. Right. Well, did you by chance happen to *eat* it yet? Uh-huh. *(Glances at TRICIA, hopeful:)* You have half of it left? Well, that's good. Because, well, you see, when I was making my pies, day b'fore yest'day, well, y'see, I made twelve of 'em, four for Tricia's wedding and eight for the bake sale—what? Oh, it's going to be a lovely wedding. She looks so beautiful. Really beautiful— *(TRICIA motions, "get to the point!")* Well, as I was sayin' ... it just so happens that I was making them over at Tricia's house and, well, she let me try on her wedding ring on while I was bakin' and it was really busy around this place as you can imagine, what with gettin' ready for the wedding and all, and we just didn't realize until, like, fifteen minutes ago, but somehow her wedding ring seems to have sort of fallen off my finger into one of the pies but we don't know which one—although we think it might be yours. *(Pause.)* Uh-huh? Uh-huh? Uh-huh. *(Pause.)* Oh. Well, now I don't think we need to go and do something like *that*, do we? No, now listen—just rake through it with a fork and see if there's a ring in there, that's all I'm asking! If you want, I'll come over there and do it myself. *(Pause.)* I will make you another pie, my goodness, what is the big deal! *(Pause.)* Well, *did* you? So then why are you threatening to SUE me if nobody swallowed it? Look—. I know! I know, just — OOH!! YOU ARE SUCH A MEAN OLD WOMAN!!! I HOPE IT *IS* IN THERE AND I HOPE YOU CHOKE ON IT AND FALL OVER DEAD AND DIE!!!

(CHARLENE slams down the phone, turns pale.) Oh, my goodness. I can't believe I just said that to Crayola Rutherford! I told her to fall over dead and die! She is the meanest woman in this whole entire town. They say when she was a girl she used to set stray cats on fire!

TRICIA. What'd she say?

CHARLENE. Oh. Well, she said she was gonna sue me, and she said she didn't want me comin' over there to look through her pie, that I wasn't "high class" enough to set foot in her house, unless of course I wanted work as her maid! Oooh!

TRICIA. Okay, then. Who's next?

CHARLENE. What?

TRICIA. Who's next? C'mon! Keep calling! I'm supposed to be down there in 45 minutes for pictures!

CHARLENE. Oh. Ah ... *(Pause.)* I'm sorry. I've gone blank.

TRICIA. THINK!

CHARLENE. Okay, okay. *(She strains to remember; then:)* Archibald Stokes!

TRICIA. Old Mr. Stokes? Owns the shoe shop?

CHARLENE. Mm-hmm.

TRICIA. Call!

(CHARLENE dials the phone, waits a moment. Someone answers.)

CHARLENE. Hello? Mr. Stokes? Well, is he there? *(Then, alarmed:)* Gone WHERE? To—? *(To TRICIA)* Oh, my goodness!

TRICIA. What?

CHARLENE. *(Waving at TRICIA to be quiet:)* How long ago was this? Uh-huh. Uh-huh. He--what? When? Oh, my Lord! *(Pause.)* Who, ME? I'm—I'm—nobody! 'Bye!

(CHARLENE slams down the phone, TRICIA at her side. CHARLENE is hyperventilating.)

TRICIA. What is it?

CHARLENE. *(Trying to catch her breath)* Oh, my goodness, oh my goodness!

TRICIA. What?

CHARLENE. Archibald Stokes was settin' down at the supper table eatin' his dessert last night when all of a sudden he just turned blue and fell over. They called an ambulance and rushed him to the hospital, but they don't know if he's gonna live!

TRICIA. They don't KNOW?

CHARLENE. No.

TRICIA. Don't know if he's gonna LIVE?

CHARLENE. No.

TRICIA. Oh, my Lord! My wedding ring killed Archibald Stokes!

CHARLENE. My PIE killed Archibald Stokes!

(Pause; they look at each other; their eyes widen as they both get the same thought at the same time:)

TRICIA. YOU killed Archibald Stokes!

CHARLENE. NO!

TRICIA. You did!

CHARLENE. Hold on! He's not dead yet! And besides, we don't know for sure if he was eating my pie when he turned blue.

TRICIA. Well, he bought the pie yesterday afternoon and then he choked to death last night, so go figure it out!

CHARLENE. They didn't say he was eating PIE. They just said ... dessert. I mean, he's an old man; maybe he was eating Jello or something! Maybe it was Jello with fruit in it and he choked on a pineapple chunk!

TRICIA. Well ... there's only one thing to do now.

CHARLENE. I know! *(But she doesn't)* What?

TRICIA. We've got to go down there.

CHARLENE. Down where?

TRICIA. To the hospital.

CHARLENE. Tricia—!

TRICIA. We've got to go down there and if he's still alive, you've got to tell him what you did to him!

CHARLENE. But you're getting married in an hour and a half.

TRICIA. So we'll *hurry*! We gotta go down there and see. We gotta! Look, I'm sure it'll be fine. They probably pumped his stomach out and they'll hand us a plastic bag with a bunch of digested hot dogs and my ring in it and it'll all be over!

CHARLENE. Yech!

TRICIA. Well, what else can we do?

CHARLENE. I don't know ...

TRICIA. Charlene, I think this may be a major turning point for you. Maybe this is your chance to face up to things, to take control of your life and be responsible for yourself. You've always been so ... careless. I think this will turn out to be a milestone for you.

CHARLENE. What if he dies?

TRICIA. Then it'll be an even *bigger* milestone.

CHARLENE. Oh, my goodness. What if they charge me with fifth degree murder, or something?

TRICIA. They won't.

CHARLENE. They might.

TRICIA. Not if we speak up *now*. It was an accident. An innocent, stupid, moronic accident.

CHARLENE. Maybe you're right ...

TRICIA. You'll only fall into a mess of trouble if you try to hide it. Like Martha Stewart.

CHARLENE. But how do we know that it was my pie? Your ring could be in Crayola Rutherford's, or Cleta Mae Dorsey's, or—

TRICIA. That's why we gotta go down there. We gotta find out. Now get your coat.

(Pause. CHARLENE does.)

CHARLENE. And you'll be with me?
TRICIA. I'll be with you.
CHARLENE. Promise?
TRICIA. I promise.
CHARLENE. Tricia?
TRICIA. Hmm?
CHARLENE. That really is a beautiful dress.

(BLACKOUT)

END OF SCENE ONE

Scene 2

(SETTING: Suggestion of a hospital room; a bed and an end table.
AT RISE: ARCHIBALD STOKES, a kindly old man, lies on the bed.
He's connected to an I.V. and some other wires. He is asleep as
TRICIA and CHARLENE enter.)

    CHARLENE. Well ... there he is.
    TRICIA. Yep. There he is.

(They both sigh relief in unison.)

    CHARLENE. Well ... at least he's not dead.
    TRICIA. No, thank goodness.

(They creep into the room a bit, cautiously observe STOKES.)

    CHARLENE. *(Whispers:)* Do you think it's still inside him?
    TRICIA. *(Whispers:)* I don't know.
    CHARLENE. Or do you think the doctors took it out?
    TRICIA. I dunno ...
    CHARLENE. I'll bet the doctors probably got it out. Don't you
think?
    TRICIA. I dunno ...

(Pause.)

    CHARLENE. What do we do now?
    TRICIA. Ask him.
    CHARLENE. ASK him?
    TRICIA. Sure.
    CHARLENE. I'm not gonna ASK him! YOU ask him! It's your
ring!
    TRICIA. But it was your pie!
    CHARLENE. It was an ACCIDENT!
    TRICIA. ASK HIM!

(TRICIA means business, and CHARLENE knows it. Slowly, reluctantly, she turns to face her victim.)

CHARLENE. Mr. Stokes? *(STOKES does not answer, but emits a wheezing sound.)* Ooh, that was creepy! I don't think he can talk; he's got about a million wires hooked up to him.
TRICIA. Mr. Stokes?

(No answer.)

CHARLENE. See? Let's go—

(TRICIA stops her.)

TRICIA. No. You stay here with him.
CHARLENE. Stay HERE? BY MYSELF?
TRICIA. I'm going to go talk to the nurses.
CHARLENE. And what, I'm going to be here ALONE with him?
TRICIA. Yes.
CHARLENE. Let me go!
TRICIA. He's ALIVE, Charlene! What're you afraid of?
CHARLENE. What if he *dies* while I'm in here?
TRICIA. Listen. I am going to the nurse's station. Will you just be still and STAY WITH THE MAN?
CHARLENE. Do you still love me?
TRICIA. NO!

(TRICIA goes. Pause. CHARLENE creeps closer to Stokes' bed, towards a chair on the other side of the room. She clings to the wall as she moves, trying to stay as far away from STOKES as possible. Silence. She eases down into the chair. Time passes. She's nervous. She can't stand the silence.)

CHARLENE. Well ... *(Long pause)* How're you today, Mr. Stokes? *(No answer, of course.)* Well, that's a stupid question, isn't it? You got about fifty miles of hoses connected to you and you almost died— *(She stops herself. Pause.)* Look. Can I get you anything? Would you like to watch TV, or—? *(No answer)* No. I guess not ... *(Pause.)* Well, then, here. Let me move these flowers up closer to you, so's you can see 'em ... *(She crosses to the beside table, slides a flower arrangement to the edge of the table so that it's closer to him. Just as she does so, he gasps loudly. This scares her and she knocks over the flowers and the vase shatters. She scrambles to pick them up.)* Oh, my goodness! Please don't die while I'm here, Mr. Stokes! Please, please, *please* don't die!

(A NURSE enters.)

NURSE. Excuse me.

CHARLENE. Yes?

NURSE. What are you doing in here?

CHARLENE. Just ... fixin' the flowers. *(Tries to reassemble the mess of broken vase, strewn flowers, etc.)* There. That's better ...

NURSE. Who are you?

CHARLENE. Me? I dunno ...

NURSE. You don't know?

CHARLENE. No ma'am.

NURSE. Are you family?

CHARLENE. Ah ...

NURSE. —Because only family are allowed in here.

CHARLENE. Yes ma'am. I'm family!

NURSE. You are?

CHARLENE. Yes ma'am.

NURSE. Well then ... if you're family ... then maybe you wouldn't mind seeing if you can get him to *eat* something.

(NURSE wheels in a patient food-serving tray with an awful-looking meal on it.)

CHARLENE. Oh ...

NURSE. He hasn't eaten anything since he got here last night. Hasn't hardly moved. Why don't you see if he'll let you feed him. *(CHARLENE just stares)* Since you're *family* ...

CHARLENE. Oh. Well ...   *(Pause; CHARLENE picks up a spoon, collects some applesauce in it, moves the spoon slowly towards STOKES' mouth with a shaking hand. Trying to smile:)* Mm-mmmm ...

NURSE. *(Just as the spoon reaches his mouth:)* Hold it! Right

there!
  CHARLENE. *(Startled:)* What?!

(NURSE frightens CHARLENE so that she drops the food on Stokes' face.)

  NURSE. You have to put a bib on him.
  CHARLENE. Oh—?
  NURSE. Yes.
  CHARLENE. A bib?
  NURSE. Yes.
  CHARLENE. Oh ... *(Sees one on the tray, obeys)* Of course.
  NURSE. There. That's better.
  CHARLENE. Yes, it is. Looks like he's sittin' in a reg'lar ol' lobster house or something!

(Pause; NURSE is confused.)

  NURSE. What?
  CHARLENE. Nothing ...
  NURSE. I'll come back and see how you're doing.
  CHARLENE. Okay.
  NURSE. T.L.C., remember. *(CHARLENE stares, blankly.)* Tender. Loving. Care.
  CHARLENE. Oh! T.L.C.! Of course! Nothin' but! *(CHARLENE caresses his face. He makes his awful gagging sound again. Sort of like a death rattle. CHARLENE smiles, shrugs. NURSE eyes CHARLENE for a moment, then shakes her head, goes. As soon as she's out of the room, CHARLENE backs away from STOKES, disgusted.)* Oooogh!

(TRICIA rushes in, sees CHARLENE against the wall.)

  TRICIA. What happened?
  CHARLENE. My heart almost stopped!
  TRICIA. What did he do?
  CHARLENE. He made this awful choking sound and he like to scared me to death! Did you find out anything?
  TRICIA. No; his doctor's off duty.

CHARLENE. Well, he won't talk to me. He just gurgles.

TRICIA. Look down his throat.

CHARLENE. What?

TRICIA. Look down his throat, see if the ring is lodged in there.

CHARLENE. I am not prying his mouth open!

TRICIA. I will, then. I'll hold it open and you look inside.

CHARLENE. Tricia!

TRICIA. Do it! Now! *(They do so.)* See anything?

CHARLENE. Not really ... it's kinda dark down there. Can you hold him up near the light more? *(They hoist him into an awkward position, CHARLENE pulling his head. She takes her hand away and, to her dismay, there's a hairpiece stuck to it.)* Aah! Oh, my goodness!!!

TRICIA. What?

CHARLENE. His HAIR came off!

TRICIA. I didn't know he was bald ...

CHARLENE. Oh, my goodness, oh my goodness ...

TRICIA. Put it back on!

CHARLENE. I can't! It's stuck! It's stuck to my HAND!

TRICIA. Shhh! Will you be quiet? You're getting hysterical!

CHARLENE. *(Pulling it off, holding it at arm's length)* Ugh!

TRICIA. Shhh!

CHARLENE. *(Whispered)* I'm sorry! But this is so gross!

TRICIA. The nurses' station is right outside!

CHARLENE. I said I'm sorry!

(CHARLENE puts the hairpiece back on, tries to adjust it. It looks pretty bad, no matter what she does to it. She finally waves it off and the two women breathe, exhausted, in silence for a moment.)

TRICIA. Did you see anything?

CHARLENE. No.

TRICIA. Let me try.

CHARLENE. Let's just go.

TRICIA. I want that ring!

CHARLENE. I'll buy you another one!

TRICIA. You can't buy me a new one! It was Andrew's great-grandmother's. It's been in his family for years. It's priceless! Now, look ... we're here now, we've got him propped up in the bed, I might as well take a look!

CHARLENE. What if the nurse comes back?

TRICIA. We'll deal with it. Here. Hold his mouth open. *(CHARLENE does. TRICIA peers down his throat.)* Holy cow!

CHARLENE. What?

TRICIA. I think I see it!

CHARLENE. No!

TRICIA. Yeah. There's something glittery down in there ...

CHARLENE. Really?

TRICIA. Yeah.

CHARLENE. Unless it's a pacemaker or something.

TRICIA. It's not a pacemaker ...

CHARLENE. Oh my goodness, Tricia! Don't yank out his pacemaker, please! I'm beggin' you!

TRICIA. What would a pacemaker be doing down somebody's throat? It's not a pacemaker ... *(Looks at CHARLENE:)* It's a *ring*!

(The NURSE enters, studies the situation. Here we have two young women holding an old man half-sitting in an awkward position with their fingers down his throat.)

NURSE. Ahem. *(TRICIA and CHARLENE look up.)* Is everything all right in here?

CHARLENE. Yes ma'am. We're just ... flossing. *(NURSE goes.)* You saw the ring? (TRICIA nods.) You're kidding!

TRICIA. Nope.

CHARLENE. *Your* ring?

TRICIA. No, he's got about six or seven other ones down there—of course it's my ring!

CHARLENE. I don't understand why the doctors didn't get it out.

TRICIA. Who knows. There's a license plate and half a dozen pop bottle tops down there too. *(CHARLENE looks at her.)* I'm just kidding!

CHARLENE. It's not funny! *(Pause.)* Well, it is ... sort of ...

(They start to giggle. CHARLENE tries to talk, can't stop giggling. Finally, TRICIA becomes sober with this thought:)

TRICIA. We've got to get it out somehow.

CHARLENE. Oh. *(But how?)* Can you reach it?

TRICIA. No, it's kinda far down there ...

(TRICIA looks around for assistance.)

CHARLENE. What're you lookin' for?

TRICIA. Is there a coat hanger or something around here?

CHARLENE. I don't see one.

TRICIA. Look in the closet. *(CHARLENE does.)* See one?

CHARLENE. No ... they're all connected to the pole.

TRICIA. You're kidding.

CHARLENE. I can't get 'em out; they're all connected, like at the Holiday Inn.

TRICIA. I hate that. Every time I travel!

CHARLENE. I know. They should be a little more trusting, don't you think? I mean, who's gonna steal your coat hangers for goodness' sake?

TRICIA. Well, help me sit him up more.

CHARLENE. Sit him up?

TRICIA. Yeah.

CHARLENE. What for?

TRICIA. We're gonna burp him.

CHARLENE. What ... ?

TRICIA. We weren't kids for nothing. Remember that time when you swallowed the tablespoon?

CHARLENE. Yeah ...

TRICIA. How do you think Mom got it out? We made you spit it up.

CHARLENE. Oh ...

TRICIA. Here. I'll hold him up ... and you pat him on the back. *(They do. CHARLENE pats him softly.)* Well, you gotta do it harder than *that. (She does.)* Harder! C'mon! Make him spit it out!

CHARLENE. I can't!

TRICIA. Why not?

CHARLENE. I'm afraid I'll hurt him!

TRICIA. You won't!

CHARLENE. I might!

TRICIA. You won't hurt him any worse than you already have! Trust me! *(CHARLENE hits him again, harder this time. But not hard enough.)* Not like that, like THIS—!

(TRICIA whacks him hard. His hairpiece falls off, landing on the floor and both women reach to get it, letting him go. He slides off the bed and rolls onto the floor. The NURSE enters.)

NURSE. What on earth are you doing to this man?!

CHARLENE. He, ah ... he wanted to get some exercise!

NURSE. Who is that?

CHARLENE. My sister.

NURSE. Your sister?

CHARLENE. Yes ma'am.

NURSE. *(To TRICIA)* Are you related to the patient?

TRICIA. *Ah ... (Looks to CHARLENE for an answer; CHAR-LENE nods.)* Yes ma'am. I am.

NURSE. *(Suspicious)* I'm sorry. I'm afraid I'm gonna have to ask you both to leave.

CHARLENE. But—

TRICIA. We just got here!

NURSE. Visiting hours are over.

CHARLENE. But he needs our help!

NURSE. He has got the best medical care anyone could afford. *(Gestures to the door.)* Please?

CHARLENE. Look, you don't understand—

NURSE. f you don't leave right this minute, I will have to call Security.

CHARLENE. HE SWALLOWED A RING, ALL RIGHT?!!

(Pause.)

NURSE. What?

TRICIA. Charlene—

NURSE. Just now?

CHARLENE. YESTERDAY! THAT'S WHY HE'S HERE! Are you people morons, or what? You can SEE it, for crying out loud, it's right there, lodged in his esophagus! It's HER ring but it's all MY FAULT and it's stuck in his throat and we *have* to get it out or I'll positively wreck her whole entire WEDDING! So, will you please give us a MINUTE? We are TRYING TO GET IT OUT!!!

(STOKES suddenly makes a loud burping/choking sound and spits the

*ring out. It lands in the center of the stage and all the women
stare at it. Then, they slowly turn their focus to him. He rises,
slowly, a little wobbly, then gets his balance and stands there,
offering a benign smile to all present.)*

STOKES. Excuse me?
NURSE. Yes sir?
STOKES. Is there a vending machine here?
NURSE. Vending machine?
STOKES. Yes.
NURSE. You want a—a vending machine?
STOKES. Yes. I'd like a Zagnut.
NURSE. A what?
STOKES. Zagnut bar. You know. Candy bar. Could you show
me where I could get a Zagnut bar and a Mr. Pibb?
NURSE. Right, ah ... right down the hall—?
STOKES. Thank you.

*(He nods a greeting to CHARLENE and TRICIA, then exits, his rear
end showing in the opening of the tie-around hospital gown.
NURSE, puzzled, watches him go, then looks at CHARLENE and
TRICIA, who shrug, and NURSE runs after STOKES.)*

NURSE. Mr. Stokes? Mr. Stokes—!

*(NURSE is gone. CHARLENE and TRICIA are now alone. CHAR-
LENE goes to the ring, picks it up.)*

CHARLENE. Wow.
TRICIA. Charlene. I'm proud of you.
CHARLENE. Why? Because I almost killed this poor man?
TRICIA. No; because you stood up to that woman. You stood up
and told the truth. All your life, you've been afraid to take responsibil-
ity, and now, I think somehow this experience will prove to be a turning point for you. I think you'll learn and grow from what happened
here today. I think you'll be a much, much more responsible person in
the future.
CHARLENE. You really think so?
TRICIA. Yeah; I really do.

CHARLENE. Wow ...
TRICIA. Now. Give me my ring back. We gotta get down there if I'm gonna get married today.

(CHARLENE hands it over. TRICIA looks at it. Pause.)

TRICIA. *(Very serious:)* Charlene.
CHARLENE. What?
TRICIA. This isn't my ring.

(They look at each other. They laugh. She's kidding.)

CHARLENE. Oh, Tricia ... you're so bad! *(TRICIA's smile fades. She's not kidding.)* Tricia—? That's the ring he spit up.
TRICIA. I know. I know it is. But it's not my ring. Look at it. My ring has a little diamond and two sapphires on it. Remember?
CHARLENE. *(Looking at it, scared now:)* Yeah ...
TRICIA. This one has two rubies.

(In unison, they look at each other ... then down at the ring, then back at each other. They suddenly let out simultaneous SCREAMS.)
BLACKOUT)

THE PLAY IS OVER.

Also by
Jason Milligan...

All's Well that Ends Swell
... And the Rain Came to Mayfield
Actors Write for Actors
Any Friend of Percy D'Angelino Is a Friend of Mine
The Best Warm Beer in Brooklyn
Both Sides of the Story
Can't Buy Me Love
Clara and the Gambler
Class of '77
Cross Country
Encore!
Exodus from McDonaldland
Family Values
The Genuine Article
Getting Even
Going Solo
His & Hers
Instincts
John's Ring
Juris Prudence
Less Said, the Better
Life After Elvis
Lullaby
Men in Suits
Money Talks
New York Stories: Five Plays About Life in New York
Next
Next Tuesday
Nights in Hohokus
The Prettiest Girl in Lafayette County
The Quality of Boiled Water
Rivals
Road Trip
Shoes
Shore Leave
Spit in Yazoo
Strange as It May Seem ...
Waiting for Ringo
Walking on the Moon
Willy Wallace Chats ... with the Kids

Please visit our website **samuelfrench.com** for complete
descriptions and licensing information.

OTHER TITLES AVAILABLE FROM SAMUEL FRENCH

ALL'S WELL THAT ENDS SWELL

Jason Milligan

Every actor knows that the secret to a successful audition is finding the perfect monologue – one that seems as if it were written exclusively for you! Mr. Milligan is our foremost author of original audition material, having already written or co-written *Actors Write for Actors, Encore, Going Solo, His & Hers, Next!* and *Both Sides of the Story*. In this, his latest volume, he has created 50 new audition pieces (25 for men and 25 for women, all various character types and situations). Each monologue comes with two possible endings – for a total of 100 variations. But Mr. Milligan goes one step further by giving you an opportunity, if you wish, to create your very own ending! He provides you with clear, concise guidelines that will help you craft your own customized conclusions! In this way, the collection provides an infinite source of possibilities for variety, spontaneity and individuality.

WALKING ON THE MOON

Jason Milligan

10m, 6f / Simply suggested sets

Twenty years ago, astronaut Chad Williams accidently ran over a crew member with the lunar rover during a mission, leaving his colleague in a coma. Racked by guilt and shame, he is reduced to doing commercials for "the carpet so soft you'll swear you're walking on the moon." Now he has a chance at the big time; all he has to do is run over his comatose friend again to vault himself into the headlines. *Walking on the Moon* was originally presented as a staged reading featuring Burt Reynolds and Joe Mantegna.

"A scathing parody of the dark side of human nature. The laughs and ridicule are plentiful, and the satire on target."
– *Los Angeles Times*

"Sharp and winning, packed with lovely absurdist details.... A pure pleasure."
– *Entertainment Today*

"A sparkling comedy."
– *Beverly Hills News*

Winner of the Southeastern Theatre Conference's 1995 Charles M.
– *Getchell New Play Award*

www.ingramcontent.com/pod-product-compliance
Lightning Source LLC
Chambersburg PA
CBHW070641120726
47909CB00004B/1525